APEX PREDATORS
of the Amazon Rain Forest

MW01155118

Arapaima

by Ellen Lawrence

Consultant:

Lesley de Souza, PhD
Conservation Scientist and Arapaima Researcher
Field Museum of Natural History
Chicago, Illinois

BEARPORT
PUBLISHING

New York, New York

Credits

Cover, © Aleksander Kurganov/Shutterstock, © Vladimir Wrangel/Shutterstock, and © Kichigin/Shutterstock; 4, © National Geographic Creative/Alamy; 5, © Lesley de Souza; 6T, © Vladimir Wrangel/Shutterstock; 6B, © Pete Oxford/Minden Pictures/FLPA; 7, © Pete Oxford/Minden Pictures/FLPA; 8T, © Filipe Frazao/Shutterstock; 8B, © Cosmographics; 9, © Photo Researchers/FLPA; 10, © Amazon-Images MBSI/Alamy; 11, © Piotr Wawrzyniuk/Dreamstime; 12T, © hypotekyfidler/iStock; 12B, © MarclSchauer/Shutterstock; 13, © Kichigin/Shutterstock and © Ammit Jack/Shutterstock; 14, © guentermanaus/Shutterstock; 15, © epa european pressphoto agency/Alamy; 15T, © RBG Kew; 16, © Aleksandr Kurganov/Shutterstock; 17, © Tennessee Aquarium; 18–19, © Kichigin/Shutterstock and © Ammit Jack/Shutterstock; 20T, © Franco Banfi/Biosphoto; 20B, © Andrew M. Allport/Shutterstock; 21, © Aleksander Kurganov/Shutterstock; 22, © Ruby Tuesday Books; 23TL, © Ammit Jack/Shutterstock; 23TC, © Photo Researchers/FLPA; 23TR, © Ondrej Prosicky/Shutterstock; 23BL, © Santi Rodriguez/Shutterstock; 23BC, © Fotos593/Shutterstock; 23BR, © Edward007/Shutterstock.

Publisher: Kenn Goin
Senior Editor: Joyce Tavolacci
Creative Director: Spencer Brinker
Photo Researcher: Ruby Tuesday Books Ltd

Library of Congress Cataloging-in-Publication Data

Names: Lawrence, Ellen, 1967– author.
Title: Arapaima / by Ellen Lawrence.
Description: New York, New York : Bearport Publishing Company, Inc., [2017] |
  Series: Apex predators of the amazon rain forest | Audience: Ages 5–8. |
  Includes bibliographical references and index.
Identifiers: LCCN 2016044533 (print) | LCCN 2016046867 (ebook) | ISBN
  9781684020331 (library) | ISBN 9781684020850 (ebook) | ISBN 978-1-64280-742-4 (pbk.)
Subjects: LCSH: Arapaima—Juvenile literature. | Freshwater fishes—Juvenile
  literature.
Classification: LCC QL624 .L39 2017 (print) | LCC QL624 (ebook) | DDC
  597.176—dc23
LC record available at https://lccn.loc.gov/2016044533

For more information, write to Bearport Publishing, 5357 Penn Avenue South, Minneapolis MN 55419. Printed in the United States of America.

Contents

River Monster

It's nighttime in the Amazon **rain forest**.

Something huge is lurking in a muddy river.

The enormous **predator** is 10 feet (3 m) long and covered with silvery scales.

What is this giant creature?

It's an arapaima (*ar*-uh-PAHY-muh)—one of the largest freshwater fish on Earth!

an arapaima

How would you describe an arapaima to someone who has never seen this giant fish?

scientists holding an arapaima

The arapaima can weigh more than 400 pounds (181 kg). That's about as much as an adult lion!

5

Meet a Mega Fish

An arapaima's giant body is **streamlined** for moving through the water.

It has a flat head and a big, upturned mouth.

The fish's body is covered with huge scales.

A single scale can be more than 2 inches (5 cm) long—that's the length of a chicken's egg!

The scales near the fish's tail have bright red edges.

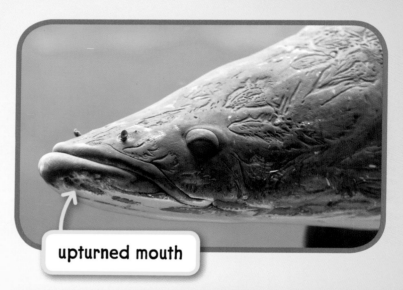

upturned mouth

scale

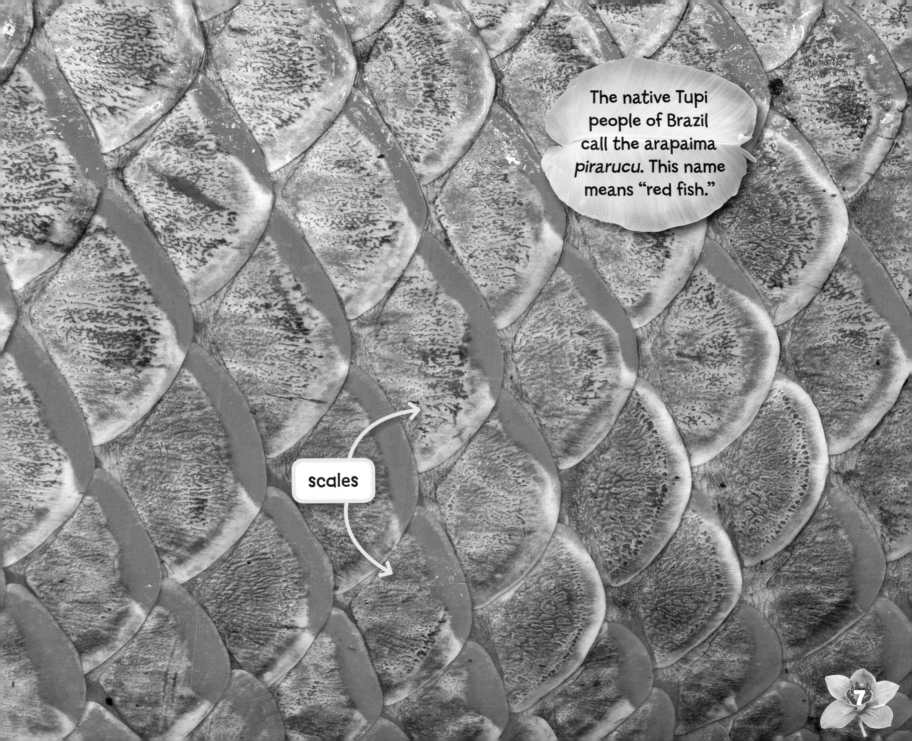

The native Tupi people of Brazil call the arapaima *pirarucu*. This name means "red fish."

scales

Watery Home

Arapaimas make their homes in the Amazon rain forest in South America.

They live in rivers, ponds, and lakes.

Every year during the wet season, lots of rain falls.

This causes the water in the rivers to rise and cover nearby land.

The fish then swim into the flooded jungle to search for food.

flooded land in the Amazon rain forest

Atlantic Ocean

Pacific Ocean

South America

N
W   E
S

■ Rivers where arapaimas live

▨ Flooded land

--- Amazon rain forest

An Unusual Fish

Most fish take in the **oxygen** they need to survive from water.

Arapaimas, however, can get oxygen from the air!

Sometimes the flooded land where they often live dries up and the water becomes shallow.

When this happens, it's difficult for most fish to stay alive.

Arapaimas, however, can survive because they breathe air.

an arapaima taking a breath

Arapaimas swim to the water's surface every 10 to 20 minutes to take a big gulp of air.

What kind of food do you think an arapaima eats?

an arapaima in shallow water

11

Watch Out!

An arapaima shares its Amazon home with around 3,000 different types of fish.

Any of them, including piranhas and catfish, can easily become a meal for an arapaima.

The big predator swims toward its **prey** with an open mouth.

Then, just like a vacuum cleaner, it sucks the fish into its huge mouth!

piranha

long-whiskered catfish

Arapaimas mostly catch fish that are swimming close to the water's surface.

13

Thousands of Teeth

An arapaima has a hard, bony tongue that's covered with thousands of sharp teeth.

The roof of the fish's mouth is also covered with teeth.

Once an animal is inside the arapaima's mouth, there's no escape.

The predator tears apart its meal with its hard, spiky tongue.

It can also crush it prey between its tongue and the roof of its mouth.

water lily leaf

Arapaimas sometimes eat water birds, frogs, and crayfish. The large fish often spend time under water lilies, waiting for food.

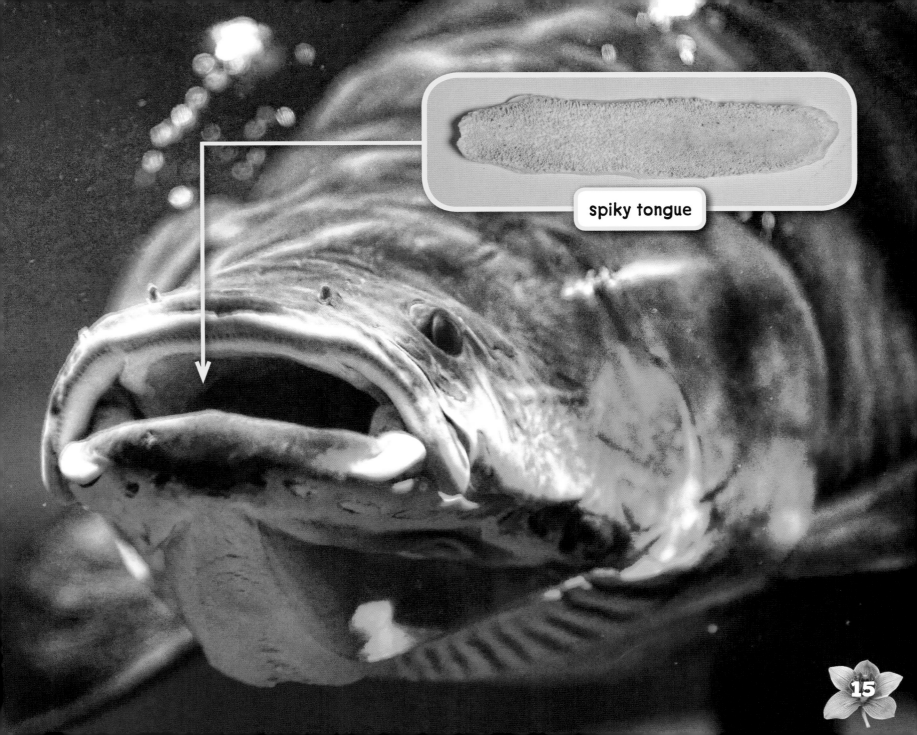

spiky tongue

15

An Underwater Nest

During February and March, adult arapaimas meet up to have young.

First, the fish use their **fins** to make an underwater nest hole in the mud.

Next, the female lays up to 20,000 eggs in the nest.

The parent arapaimas protect their eggs by chasing away other fish that try to eat them.

After about three months, tiny babies, called fry, hatch from the eggs.

a pair of arapaimas

Many animals, including birds, caimans, and other fish, eat baby arapaimas. How do you think the parent fish protect their babies?

Protective Parents

Once the fry hatch from their eggs, they swim close to their father's head.

The mother arapaima swims around the father and babies to keep predators away.

If a predator gets too close, however, the father sucks the fry into his mouth!

Then he carries them to a safe place far away from danger.

A mother and father arapaima release a milky-looking liquid from their heads into the water. Scientists think it might be food for the babies, but no one knows for sure.

baby arapaimas

Top Predators

By the time they are three months old, arapaima fry are about 35 inches (89 cm) long.

The young fish leave their parents to live on their own.

Big anacondas and caimans may try to eat the little arapaimas.

However, once they are fully grown adults, arapaimas are top, or apex, predators.

They are too big for any other animals to hunt them!

anaconda

caiman

Arapaimas keep growing throughout their lives. Scientists don't know for sure how long they live, but it might be as long as 50 years.

Science Lab

Help the Arapaimas!

Arapaimas are in danger of becoming extinct in their Amazon home. Why?

- People have caught too many of the fish for food.

- People are turning the flooded land where arapaimas live into farmland.

- People mine for gold and drill for oil. This creates harmful pollution that flows into the arapaimas' river home.

Use books and the Internet to learn more about why these big fish are endangered.

Then make your own book to tell friends and family members about what you've learned.

Make an Arapaima Book

1. Have an adult staple three pieces of paper together.

2. On each page, write a fact and draw pictures that explain the ways in which arapaimas are at risk.

3. Share your book with friends and family.

Science Words

fins (FINZ) flat body parts that fish use for swimming and steering

oxygen (OK-suh-juhn) an invisible gas found in air and water that animals need to breathe

predator (PRED-uh-tur) an animal that hunts other animals for food

prey (PRAY) an animal that is hunted and eaten by another animal

rain forest (RAYN FOR-ist) a large area of land covered with trees and other plants where lots of rain falls

streamlined (STREEM-lined) shaped to easily move through water

Index

Read More

Lynette, Rachel. *Piranhas (Monsters of the Animal Kingdom).* New York: Rosen (2013).

Martin, Isabel. *Fish (A Question and Answer Book).* North Mankato, MN: Capstone (2015).

Owen, Ruth. *Monster Fish (It's A Fact! Real-Life Reads).* New York: Ruby Tuesday Books (2014).

Learn More Online

To learn more about arapaimas, visit
www.bearportpublishing.com/ApexPredators

About the Author

Ellen Lawrence lives in the United Kingdom. Her favorite books to write are those about nature and animals. In fact, the first book Ellen bought for herself, when she was six years old, was the story of a gorilla named Patty Cake that was born in New York's Central Park Zoo.